Devil for Sale

by

E. E. Richardson

First published in 2007 in Great Britain by
Barrington Stoke Ltd
18 Walker Street, Edinburgh EH3 7LP

www.barringtonstoke.co.uk

ISBN: 978-1-84299-462-7

Printed in Great Britain by Bell & Bain Ltd

A Note from the Author

A few years ago, a friend told me about a box that was for sale on the internet. People said there was a curse on it. No one was sure if it was for real or a fake. The seller said the box had given them bad luck. They just wanted to get rid of it.

That started me thinking. What if something was under a curse ... And what if the only safe way to get rid of it was to sell it? How would you get someone to buy it? Would you have to trick them? And what if someone had tricked you first?

That's how I came up with Ben's story ...

Contents

Chapter 1

The Man at the Car Boot Sale

Ben didn't want to be there.

Car boot sales were boring as hell. They only ever sold total junk. He'd wanted to stay at home, but his mum had nagged him. She'd gone on and on until he'd felt he had to come with her.

"It's your old toys we're selling, Ben!" his mum had said.

So what? It wasn't like she needed help to sell them. Once the table was set up, he had nothing to do.

So he went for a walk around the cars and tables. It didn't take him too long. Ben could see right away there was nothing he wanted to buy. Why waste his time looking any closer?

He got to the last stall before anyone else did.

He almost didn't bother going over. The table was all by itself in a new row, and Ben was getting thirsty. He was about to go back for a drink when he noticed something odd.

There was only one thing left on the table.

Ben frowned. Had the man sold a load of stuff already? Or had he only got one thing with him to sell? It was weird. Ben drifted over to get a better look.

The man didn't look like a brilliant salesman. In fact, he looked sweaty and nervous. He had a black eye and a puffy lip, as if he'd been in a fight.

The last thing left on his table was an odd statue. It was a funny little fat man made of dull grey metal. It had a grin as wide as its face, and narrow eyes.

Ben thought it was ugly. Even so, he felt as if he had to pick it up. It was heavy, but seemed to be hollow. It rattled as if it had something in it.

"People collect this sort of statue," the man said, and gave Ben a hopeful smile. "Very rare. Yours for a quid."

Ben smirked and shook his head. "No, thanks." He started to put the statue back down, but the man grabbed his wrist.

"50p. 10p. Come on, kid. Do me a favour here." The man's eyes were full of panic.

No one was that desperate to sell a bit of junk. It had to be dodgy. What was in it? Drugs or something?

Whatever it was, Ben didn't want to know.

"Sorry, mate," Ben muttered. "No money on me," he lied. He pulled his arm away. Why did you always get weirdos at boot fairs?

"Wait!" the man called out as Ben went to leave. Ben saw something roll off the table and into the grass. "Could you just pick that up for us, kid? Cheers."

Ben wanted to get away, but it seemed kind of rude to just walk off. He spotted a pound coin in the grass, and bent down to pick it up. "There you go, mate," he said as he handed it back to the man.

"Sold!" the man said quickly. He shoved the statue into Ben's hands.

"What?" Ben asked.

He tried to give the statue back, but the man wouldn't take it.

"It's yours," he insisted. "You gave me the money. It's sold. Can't take it back now."

Ben stared at him. "It was your pound!"

"Money changed hands!" The man's voice was desperate. "That means the statue's sold. Fair and square. Yours to keep." He folded up his table and shoved it in the back of his car.

"But I don't want it!" Ben said loudly.

"Nor do I," the man spat out. He jumped into his car, and backed up so fast Ben had to run out of the way.

The car roared off. Ben looked down at the statue in his hands. Now what was he going to do with it?

He didn't want to just toss it in the bin. It was interesting. Why was the man in such a rush to get rid of it? Was something hidden inside?

Ben walked back to the car with the statue. He tried to see if anything was inside it. He couldn't work out how to open it. Was there a switch he couldn't see?

"What's that you've got there, love?" his mum asked. She only gave him a quick glance. People had started to arrive and were looking at all the things she had out.

"Just something I bought," Ben said. "Can I sit in the car?"

"All right, but keep the window open. It's like an oven in there."

Ben didn't notice the heat. He was thinking too much about the statue. It was a mystery, and he planned to solve it.

There had to be a way to get inside.

Chapter 2
The Gremlin's Curse

Ben still hadn't opened up the statue by the time they got back home.

By now he was sure that the way into the statue was its mouth. He could see there was a join there. Maybe the chin dropped open, or you took the statue's head off? But no matter what Ben did, he just couldn't make the mouth slide open. His fingers were all sore from trying.

When they got in, he found his dad's tool kit. He took a screwdriver with him upstairs to his room. Maybe he could use it to force the join open. If he put the screwdriver on the edge of the statue's mouth and whacked ...

Ow!

Ben swore. The screwdriver slipped off the metal and struck his hand. It was a nasty scrape, too – bleeding like mad. He ran downstairs to get a plaster.

"What did you do?" his dad asked, as he dug in the First Aid kit.

"Oh, nothing. It's just a scratch," Ben said.

He didn't want to explain just how he'd done it. His dad would offer to help, and Ben didn't want that. After all this time trying, he wanted to do this himself.

As it turned out, he'd done it already. When he picked the statue up, its mouth fell open. It must have been knocked loose when it hit the floor.

The mouth opened just like a human jaw. Ben found it a bit creepy. He couldn't shake the feeling that the statue would bite him if he stuck his fingers inside.

That would be a stupid thing to do anyway. Who knew what might be in it? Ben turned the statue upside down and shook it.

He couldn't help but feel a buzz of excitement. What would fall out? It could be rare coins. Stolen diamonds. There might be a reward ...

What fell out was too dull to be a diamond. It just looked like a small, grey chip of stone. Ben went to pick it up, then jumped back. Not stone – it was a bit of bone! Gross.

And he'd tipped it out onto his bed. It was only the size of his fingertip, but even so. That was just nasty.

What was it doing in the statue?

Ben gave it another shake. There was something else in there, but it didn't sound hard. He tapped the bottom to knock it out.

A piece of folded paper fell out. There were some dark hairs caught up with it. Ben shook them off in disgust. God, what was this? Who would keep this sort of thing?

He unfolded the note slowly. The paper was so old, he was afraid it would crack. Written on it was a short verse.

I am the gremlin. This is mine.
Sell me, buy me, and that's fine.

I am not yours to give away.
Steal me, and I'll make you pay.

Ben felt the hairs on his arms stand up. Was this why the man had been so desperate to sell it? The words read like some sort of curse.

Ben didn't believe in black magic. Still, the idea of it made him feel uneasy. Where had the hair and bone come from? What if it was a human bone?

It was exactly the same size as his fingertip ...

It didn't matter what sort of bone it was, Ben didn't want it on his bed. But he didn't want to just tip the stuff into the bin. He'd have to put it back in the statue.

He didn't want to touch any of it, so he got a pen to poke the paper and the bone into the statue. The bit of paper got stuck. It wouldn't drop in. In the end, Ben gave up and used his fingers to push it.

As it fell inside, the statue's mouth snapped shut like a mousetrap. Ben only just pulled his hand away in time. He swore in shock and dropped the statue. He could have lost a finger!

He sat down on the bed. His heart was racing. Even if there wasn't a curse, that statue was dangerous. That was twice Ben had nearly hurt himself quite badly.

After a while, he picked the statue up and set it on his desk. It could stay up there for the moment. Right now, he didn't want to touch it more than he had to.

Once he'd calmed down a bit, Ben felt silly. It was that stupid poem that had got to him. So he'd been a bit clumsy – so what? It was the note that had made him start thinking weird things. The statue was just a chunk of metal.

Ben still wanted to get rid of it, but there was no rush. He'd just stick it in the bin next rubbish day. For now, it could stay where it was.

Ben got on with the rest of his day. He didn't think about the statue much at all. By dinner time, he'd almost forgotten he had it.

Until there was an enormous crash from upstairs.

Chapter 3
Nightmares

"What was that?" His dad looked up.

"Ben, I think that crash was in your room," his mum said.

"I'll go and have a look." Ben put his knife and fork down and headed for the stairs.

The door to his bedroom was still shut, just as he'd left it. He pushed it open and peered inside. At first, he could see nothing wrong.

Then he looked down, and saw the statue on the floor behind the door. How had it got all the way over here? The desk was up at the other end of the room.

He bent down to pick it up. As he did, Ben saw that the bottom of the door was covered in scratches. It looked as if something had tried to claw its way out.

He knew what must have happened.

"Tiger! Come on, Tiger! Where are you?" Ben whistled, and checked under the bed for the cat.

He must have shut the cat in his room by mistake before dinner. That was how the statue had got knocked down. Tiger must have panicked and cried to get out when it fell. But where was he now?

"Tiger!" Ben checked in the other upstairs rooms.

Tiger was curled up on the chair in Mum and Dad's room. He must have crept out of Ben's bedroom while Ben was looking under the bed. Now Tiger was trying to pretend that he'd been on the chair all along.

Ben went over to stroke him. "Who's a sneaky little cat, then? Did you scare yourself, you stupid thing?"

Tiger just stretched his legs and yawned. He looked dopey, as if he'd been asleep for hours. But of course, he couldn't have been.

What else could have been in Ben's room?

That night, Ben had trouble getting off to sleep. The house seemed to be full of noises. Every time he shut his eyes there was a creak or a groan or a rustle.

It was just the wind, of course. He knew that.

He still got up twice to turn the light on.

Both times, Ben couldn't help it. His eyes turned to look at the statue. He could swear that its grin had got wider. It was like it was leering at him. Ben wanted to turn it round to face the wall so he couldn't see its eyes. But that was just silly.

He made himself get back in bed. The statue wasn't staring at him. It didn't really have eyes. Ben felt stupid. It was only a bit of metal.

Five minutes later, he got up and turned it around.

Even so, it was hours before he fell asleep. When he did, he didn't feel like he was dreaming.

In his dream, Ben was still in bed, and it was still dark. There was something heavy sitting on his chest. Ben could feel short, bristly fur, and smell its breath.

It was the smell of something that was dead and rotting.

"Tiger?" Ben said and tried to push the cat off. "God, what have you been eating? Bad cat! Off the bed!"

But it wasn't Tiger.

A pair of blood-red eyes snapped open in front of his face. They were narrow, ugly slits, full of hate. The thing let out a hiss ... then it jumped.

Its sharp claws dug into the sides of Ben's neck. It was crushing his throat! He couldn't breathe.

Ben tried to throw it off, but it was too strong. He couldn't make it let go with its claws. Ben's chest was burning, and he was starting to see flashing lights ...

And then he woke up.

He lay staring up at the ceiling and panting for breath. The weight was gone from his chest. He could breathe. It had only been a dream.

Just a dream ... but his chest still hurt. He really did feel like he'd been strangled. Had he been holding his breath in his sleep?

Ben sat up and rubbed his neck. Even the skin felt sore. What had he done to himself? He got up and switched the light on to look in the mirror.

On each side of his neck, there was a line of four little red dots. It looked like he'd been stabbed with a fork.

Or by some sort of animal with claws.

Chapter 4
The Maths Lesson

By morning, the marks on Ben's skin had started to fade. His neck looked a bit red, but that was all. Had he only dreamed that they were there?

Ben could feel the statue watching him as he looked in the mirror. He was sure he'd turned it round to face the wall last night. Or had that been part of a dream, too?

He didn't like this.

The statue bothered him. Why was he keeping it? He might as well throw it away right now.

But not in the bin at home. He didn't like the idea of it sitting in there for days. He'd take it with him to school and shove it in a bin on the way.

At least, that was the plan.

The whole morning went wrong from the start. First Ben couldn't find his tie, and then his French book was lost. By the time he found them both, he was so late he had to beg his dad for a lift.

He got to school just in time to hear the late bell. He had to run like mad to make it to his first class. There was no time to worry about the statue in his bag.

It stayed in there for most of the day. But in the last lesson Ben couldn't find his maths book. In the end he tipped the whole bag out on the desk. The statue fell out on top of his books.

"What's that?" His friend Mark leaned over to see.

"It's this statue thing I got at the week-end." Ben showed it to him. "Some weird guy at a car boot sale gave it to me. He was mental! Kept trying to trick me into buying it."

"Let me see." Mark grabbed it off him. "Oh, man, that is ugly … Ow!"

He swore and dropped the statue. It bounced off the desk and onto the floor.

"Are you OK?" Ben asked.

"Yeah." Mark sucked his finger. "That thing has sharp edges. Oh, watch out." He gave Ben a nudge. "Mr White's coming."

Ben leaned down to grab the statue, but the teacher got there first. "All right, Ben," he said as he tapped the statue with a foot. "What's this, and what does it have to do with maths?"

"Er ... nothing," Ben had to say.

"That's what I thought." Mr White picked the statue up, and gave it a funny look.

"I was just about to put it away," Ben promised.

"In that case, you won't mind if I keep hold of it for you. You can have it back at the end of the lesson." Mr White moved off with the statue under his arm.

"Sorry," Mark said, once he'd gone.

"I don't care." Ben gave a shrug. "He can keep it if he likes. I don't want it." He started on the maths work.

Mr White put the statue on his desk. A few times, Ben saw him looking at it. Maybe he thought it was creepy, too.

The lesson seemed to drag on for ages. Ben was soon yawning. It was sunny in the class, and he hadn't got much rest last night. It was hard not to fall asleep in his seat.

"OK, class." Mr White stood up and clapped his hands. "You should have finished that first page by now. Who wants to come up here and solve question one?"

Ben kept his head down. He hoped Mr White wouldn't pick him. There was no way he'd get the answer right. He'd done almost no work.

The next thing he knew, there was a huge crash. There was a moment of shock, then a few people started to laugh. "Nice one, sir!" someone shouted.

But then the laughs started to fade. Ben jumped up, but so did everyone else, and he couldn't see what was going on.

He pushed past some people to get to the front. Mr White was slumped on the floor. He must have slipped, or tripped over, or ...

He was lying very still. A sort of scared hush had fallen over the class.

"Sir?" said Jenny Moss.

"Mr White?" asked someone else.

"Oh, my God," said one of the girls. Someone at the back swore. No one knew what to do.

"Oh, crap, I think his head's bleeding," Mark said suddenly.

"Someone get a teacher!" Jenny said.

"Oh, God ..." another girl said.

"Get a teacher!" A few people ran for the door.

Ben felt worse than useless. He shouldn't be just standing here – but what else could he do? There wasn't any way that he could help.

He looked down at the statue. Its mouth had been shut, but now it was open just a crack.

It almost looked like it was laughing.

Chapter 5
Mark's Idea

Mr White was taken away in an ambulance.

No one would say if he was all right or not. The other teachers just tried to get them to clear the corridor. "Come on, the bell's gone. You should all be heading home," they kept saying.

But no one really wanted to leave. They were all still a little bit stunned.

"That was freaky," Mark said. "Did you see? He just tripped over nothing. It was really weird."

"Yeah." Ben felt sick.

He couldn't stop thinking about the statue.

Steal me, and I'll make you pay …

Mr White had taken the statue off him. He would have given it back, but maybe that didn't matter. Maybe it still counted as stealing.

The statue really did have a curse on it. Ben didn't want to believe it, but it had to be true. This couldn't just be random bad luck.

"Hey, you left your statue thing behind," Mark said as they left the school. "Want to go back and get it?"

Ben shook his head grimly. "No way. I don't want to see that thing ever again."

He didn't get his wish. When he got home and opened his bag, the statue was lying on top of his books.

Ben's heart raced and he felt dizzy. He closed his eyes and counted to ten.

When he opened them, the statue was still there.

He'd left it at school. He *knew* that he'd left it at school. And yet, here it was in his bag.

It had followed him home.

Ben's chest grew tight with panic. What was he going to do? He didn't want to keep the statue. It hurt everyone who came near it.

He couldn't stop thinking about what had happened to Mr White. What if Ben had a fall like that? He was all alone in the house. He could bleed to death before his parents got home.

He couldn't stay here on his own. As soon as he'd got changed, Ben grabbed his bag and left.

He headed for Mark's house. Mark was the only one who might believe him about the curse. He'd seen what had happened to Mr White.

As soon as Mark opened the door, Ben held up the statue. "You saw me leave this at school, right?" he asked.

"Er ... yeah." Mark looked puzzled.

"This is going to sound crazy," Ben said, "but I think this thing's got a curse on it."

He told Mark the whole story.

"That does sound crazy," Mark agreed, at the end. "But yeah, that is pretty freaky."

"It's more than freaky," Ben said. "I left it at school! How am I meant to get rid of it if I can't leave it behind?"

"Burn it," Mark said. "Isn't it fire that gets rid of curses?"

"I can't burn it, it's metal." Ben knew there was no way it would melt in a normal fire.

Mark thought for a moment. "Not the statue," he said. "You need to burn the stuff inside it. The bone and hair and whatever. If you destroy that, then it's just a funny-shaped tin."

Ben gave a shrug. "I don't know ..."

Maybe if they tried to burn the stuff, that would lift the curse. Or maybe it would just make the gremlin angry.

Mark had already jumped out of his chair. "Come on. We can do it down the bottom of the garden."

Mark found some matches and opened the back door. Ben followed him down to the bottom of the garden. He was sure this was a bad idea, but he didn't know what else to do.

"This is where my dad does bonfires," Mark said. There was a patch of earth, and a heap of old wood. "The wood's pretty dry. It shouldn't be hard to get a fire going."

Mark broke off a few smaller twigs and made a pile with them. Then he took the matches out of his pocket and tried to light one.

"Ow!" He dropped the unlit match on the ground. "God." He peered at his thumb.

"Are you OK?" Ben was jumpy with nerves.

"I'm fine." Mark rubbed his hand. "I just scraped my thumb on the matchbox. Don't panic, all right?"

That was easy for Mark to say. Ben felt very nervous. "Mark, wait," he blurted out. "I don't like this."

"Oh, relax, OK?" Mark bent down to pick up the match he'd dropped. "We only need a tiny little fire. It won't take much to burn that stuff up."

He struck the match. As it caught light, Mark's hand seemed to jerk. The flame touched the side of the matchbox.

The next thing they knew, the whole box was on fire.

Chapter 6
Fire!

"What the hell?" Mark swore and let go of the box. It was a ball of fire before it hit the dirt.

It was like the cardboard had been dipped in petrol. Ben didn't think it would burn out on its own.

"Quick, stamp on it!" he said sharply.

Mark didn't move. "I've still got my school shoes on," he said.

"Mark!" Ben shouted. He knew if the fire spread, they'd have more to worry about than burnt shoes. Ben pushed him out of the way and stamped the fire out himself.

At least, he tried to. The box was crushed, but it kept on burning. As he lifted his foot, the wind swept the bits of box away. They were all over the garden before Ben could move to stop them.

Mark swore again. "The whole garden's going to catch fire!"

It had been hot for weeks, and the grass was dry as straw. If a proper blaze got started it would spread like mad in no time.

"How do we stop it?" Ben shouted, in a panic.

"I don't know, just do *something*!" Mark turned and ran towards the garden shed.

A patch of grass was starting to catch fire. Ben put that out, but by the time he had, two more fires had started. And what was that horrible smell?

He turned, and saw smoke rising from the roof of the shed. A spark must have landed up on top where he couldn't see. There was no way he'd be able to put that one out. And why was Mark still in the shed?

"Mark, get out here!" he yelled. "The shed roof's on fire. I need help!" He couldn't put all the fires out by himself.

"I'm coming!" Mark shouted back. There were crashes and bangs as he threw things around. Then he came out with a hose in his arms. "Just hold on a minute!"

He sprinted for the house.

"We haven't got long!" Ben cried. Things were out of control. Ben had put out one of the grass fires, but the other was still going. It was too big now to crush out. He'd only get burned if he tried. "Mark! Hurry up!"

"I'm coming, I'm coming!" Mark was trying to get the hose hooked up to the sink. "I've almost got it!"

He spun the tap and the hose started to spit water.

"Spray it on the shed roof!" Ben shouted. That fire was the worst. And if the whole shed went up, it would take the fence with it.

"I'm trying!" Mark was having a fight with the hose. The stream of water was too strong to aim well. Ben gasped as it struck him on the arm.

"Hey, don't point it at me!" he said. The water was so cold it stung.

"Sorry!" Mark yelled.

Mark got the hose under better control, and Ben jogged over to help him. It took a while, but at last they got all the fires out. They turned off the water, and then stood and looked at the garden.

It was a mess.

What wasn't burned was soaking wet. Some of the plants had been broken by the spray from the hose. The roof of the shed was scorched, and so were lots of patches of grass.

There was no way they could ever hide what had happened.

"We are so dead," said Ben.

"Yeah." Mark ran a hand through his hair. "Look, Ben, you might as well go."

"Oh, no." Ben shook his head. "Come on. I'm not leaving you to take all the blame." It was because of his statue they'd started the fire, after all.

"What blame?" Mark said with a weak grin. "I'll say it was a cigarette butt blown over the fence. How would they know? I'll be a hero, mate."

Ben wasn't so sure Mark's parents would buy that story. "I don't know ..." he said.

"Ben. Just go, OK?" Mark begged. "Don't worry about the garden. You've still got to deal with that statue. Get rid of it, man. It's too dangerous to keep."

"Yeah." Ben gave a sigh and went to pick up his bag.

He knew Mark was right. He just didn't think it was going to be that easy.

Chapter 7
A Trip to the Beach

The train station was a short walk from Mark's house. Instead of going home, Ben went there. He got a ticket for the last station the train went to. He'd be home late for dinner, but he didn't care. He just wanted the statue to be gone.

The train was pretty full, so Ben had to stand. He held onto the back of a seat so tightly it hurt his hand. Not that holding tight would help much, if the gremlin made the train crash.

The train slowed down and Ben's heart sped up. What was going on? Had someone set off the alarm? Maybe there was a bomb threat. Maybe the train was on fire ...

And then he saw the sign at the side of the track. They'd arrived at the last station.

Ben still couldn't relax. He knew the gremlin would find some other way to stop him. The train doors would slam. He'd slip and fall onto the tracks. His ticket would be missing so he couldn't get out.

But none of that happened.

Am I going crazy? Ben thought. Maybe there was no curse. Maybe he was just having a really bad week. Maybe it was all just a run of bad luck.

Maybe – but he was still getting rid of that statue. He wasn't going to take any chances.

The station Ben had picked was by the sea. As he walked down to the beach, there was no one else around. It wasn't dark yet, but it had got pretty windy. The tide was in, and boats were bobbing on the waves.

Ben took the statue out of his bag. It looked just the same as ever. He didn't know what he'd expected to see. A look of fear, maybe, or an angry glare?

It was just a statue. Before Ben could change his mind, he lifted his arm up and threw it into the sea.

It sank like a stone as soon as it hit the water. There weren't even any bubbles to mark the spot.

Ben felt sort of cheated. That was it? It was a bit like pulling a cracker that didn't go bang.

He watched the waves for a while, but nothing else happened. He turned and left the beach to head back home.

Ben's mobile rang while he was on the train. He saw the call was from his mother.

"Sorry, Mum," he said as he answered it. "I forgot about the time. I didn't know it was so late. I'll be home soon."

She wasn't pleased, but he didn't really care. He felt like he'd had something heavy lifted off him. The statue was gone, and that was all that mattered.

His dinner was cold, but Ben didn't mind. At least he knew he wasn't going to choke on it. As he ate, he thought about Mark.

Ben hoped Mark hadn't got in too much trouble for the fire. He didn't dare ring to find out. What if Mark's mum or dad answered? He didn't want them to find out he'd been there too. No, he'd wait and talk to Mark in the morning.

He went to bed early that evening. The wild events of the day had worn him out.

"Are you sure you're not ill?" his mum asked him. "You do look a bit pale."

"I'm fine," he insisted. "I just didn't get too much sleep last night."

"All right, then." She smiled at him. "Make sure the cat's not upstairs before you go to bed."

"Right." Ben went to check that Tiger was in his basket. As he looked in the front room, his dad stood up from his chair.

"Ah, Ben. I meant to tell you," he said. "I've got something of yours."

"Yeah?" Ben followed him out to the kitchen.

His dad nodded. "I found it out in the garden earlier. I'm sorry it's got a bit wet. I must have splashed it while I was watering. I left it out on the back step to dry off."

He opened the back door, and turned to speak to Ben again. "There you go. That *is* yours, isn't it? I saw it on your desk the other day."

It was the statue.

Chapter 8
No Sleep

Ben took the statue back upstairs with him. What else could he do?

It was obvious there was no point trying to dump it. No matter where Ben took it, it wouldn't be far enough. But he didn't see how he could destroy it. The fire had shown what would happen if he tried.

The poem had said that he was safe if he sold it. But how could he do that? Would he have to trick someone? That was what the man at the car boot sale had done to him. That was just evil. And no one would buy it off him if they knew the truth.

He was stuck with it. Stuck until it killed him.

The way things were going, that wouldn't take long.

The statue just sat there, smirking at him. In a sudden fit of rage, Ben scooped it up and threw it at the wall.

It hit with a crash that made the shelves rattle. Ben watched the row of CDs on the top shelf. He could see the end one starting to topple ...

He ran forward to catch it. He didn't see the statue roll under his feet.

Ben's foot landed right on top of it. The metal dug into his bare skin. Ben let out a yell of pain, and hopped back.

That little jump was all it took.

The CD dropped off the end of the shelf. The one next to it followed. Then the next, then the next, then the next ... It was like watching a landslide.

The CD cases shattered as they hit the floor. Bits of plastic flew all over the room. The noise was terrible. It seemed to go on for ever.

It didn't stop until there were no more CDs to fall. Ben looked down at the mess. The statue rolled to a stop in front of him.

He heard a door open downstairs. "Ben, what was that?" his dad called up.

"Don't worry! Ben yelled back. "I just knocked some CDs down!"

He let out a snort of laughter at his own words. It was either that or he'd cry.

His right foot was stinging. Ben sat down to look at it. No blood, but he could still see the dents where the metal had dug in.

There was a dent in the wall, too. The statue had scratched the paint. You could see flecks of the green that the room had been painted before.

But the statue had not been harmed at all.

Ben let out a sigh. He wanted to crawl into bed and go to sleep, but he knew he couldn't. First he had to clean up all this mess.

He just hoped the gremlin's fun was over for the night.

It took ages to pick up all of his CDs. He had to sweep the floor to get all the bits of plastic. The last thing he needed was more sharp stuff to step on.

He shut the statue away in his desk drawer. At least that way he wouldn't have to look at it. Then, at last, he switched the light off and got into bed.

Ben was worn out, but he just couldn't sleep. He kept thinking he could hear noises from the desk.

Scratch, scratch.

He knew it was just his imagination.

Scratch, scratch.

Or maybe there was a mouse. It might be coming from under the floor, not the desk drawer.

Scratch, scratch, scratch ...

He pulled the pillow up over his head.

Now it was hard to breathe. Ben rolled on to one side, then the other. He tried lying on his front. No matter what he did, he couldn't doze off. His skin felt hot and itchy, and his mouth was dry.

In the end he got up to get a drink of water. It cooled him down, but now he felt more wide awake than ever. At this rate, he was going to be up all night.

When he got back to his room, Ben could see something on the floor. He must have knocked the pillow down when he got up. He bent down to grab it.

His hand closed around warm fur. Blood-red eyes flew open, and there was a hiss.

The gremlin leapt for his throat.

Chapter 9
Where's Mark?

Ben yelled.

At least, he tried to. All that came out was a weak croak. The air was pushed out of his lungs as the thing hit his chest.

It clung on with all four sets of claws. Ben staggered back and hit his head on the wall. He tried to push the gremlin off, but he couldn't make it let go.

The gremlin was too heavy for him. He felt like he was going to snap in half. He slid down the wall and hit the floor.

The stink of the beast filled his nose. It was so foul, he could hardly breathe. Ben was starting to get dizzy. His heart was beating too fast in his chest.

The gremlin's claws dug in harder. The pain was sharp, but it seemed to come from far away. The shadows in the room were growing darker ...

He blacked out.

****

When Ben woke up, he was still on the floor. There was no sign of the gremlin. The night had turned colder, and he was starting to shiver.

At last he felt strong enough to stand. He switched the light on, and stared at himself in the mirror. His face was pale, and his T-shirt was slashed in four places.

He lifted it slowly. There were long red slash marks on his skin. One of them was still bleeding. He touched it with a finger. It was still really sore.

Had the gremlin really been in his room? Or had it been part of a dream? He didn't know. Did it matter anyway? Even if it was a dream, Ben was still hurt. He shivered as he let the T-shirt slip back down.

He wasn't even safe when he was asleep. Ben got back in bed. He felt sick.

But what else was there to do?

He didn't get much more rest that night. By the next morning he hurt all over. All of his cuts and scrapes were sore. His head was throbbing because he'd had so little sleep.

His parents both eyed him as he sat down to breakfast.

"What time did you get to bed last night?" his dad asked.

"Early. I just didn't sleep much." Ben poked his cereal with a spoon. He wasn't at all hungry.

"You're as pale as a ghost," his mum said as she felt his head. "You're not hot," she murmured. "Do you feel sick?"

"No. I'm OK." He'd have said the same thing even if he *did* feel ill. The last thing he needed now was a day off school. He didn't dare be home alone with the statue.

When he packed his bag for school, Ben put the statue in it. There was no point leaving it out. If it wanted to show up, it would. At least this way he'd know it was there from the start.

When he got to school, everyone was talking about Mr White. He hadn't come in today. Was he dead? Was he in a coma? Did he have brain damage? There were lots of different stories, but no one really knew.

Mark didn't show up either. Ben didn't think too much of it at first. He didn't start to worry until about ten to ten. Mark was late sometimes, but not this late.

He checked his phone under the desk. There were no texts, and no missed calls. If Mark was bunking off, he would have told Ben. So where was he?

A bad feeling was starting to grow inside Ben.

He should have rung Mark last night. He should have stayed with him. What if the fire hadn't been fully put out? What if Mark had breathed in too much smoke? A million things could have gone wrong.

Ben didn't go to his next lesson. As soon as the bell went, he slipped round to the back of the school. He got his phone out and rang Mark's mobile.

The mobile phone you have dialled is switched off.

Ben swore. What was it doing switched off? Mark never turned his phone off, even when he was supposed to. It was always going off when they were in class.

He tried Mark's home number. The phone rang, and rang, and rang. No one picked it up.

As he stopped the call, Ben's hands were sweating. The rest of him felt cold as ice. What could he do now?

Everyone else had gone to class. He should go too. He could try and phone again in an hour.

He could – but he wasn't going to. Ben turned to look at the side gate. It would be locked, but he could climb over it. No one was watching.

Mark could be hurt. Mark could be *dead*. How could he go back to class until he knew?

He started to run for the gate.

Chapter 10
Bad News

It took a while to get to Mark's. Ben didn't dare take the quick way down the main road. He'd be spotted for sure.

Most days that wouldn't matter. The odds were low he'd see any police, and no one else would care that he was bunking. But today wasn't most days. He was under a curse.

So he kept to the back streets. Every car that passed made him tense up. He kept waiting to hear the honk of a horn and a yell–

Hey, kid, why aren't you in school? Get back here!

But no one tried to stop him.

Ben made it to Mark's road. He let out a sigh of relief as he saw the house. It looked just the same as ever. He'd half expected to see a burned out shell.

But it didn't look like anyone was home. The car was gone, and the windows were all dark. Ben knocked on the door all the same.

No one answered.

He felt a bit lost. What did he do now? He still had no clue where Mark was. If he wasn't at home, and he wasn't at school ...

Ben tried to ring Mark's phone again. It was still switched off. He kicked the wall of the house. Where was Mark?

A voice from behind him made him jump. "You're Mark's friend, aren't you, dear?"

Ben turned to see the little old lady who lived in the next house.

"Er, yeah," he said. "Do you know where he is? He didn't turn up to school." Ben hoped she wasn't going to ask why he wasn't there either.

But she wanted to gossip, not nag. "Oh, no, dear. I'm not surprised," she said. "They'll still be at the hospital, I should think."

"The hospital?" Ben's mouth felt dry. All of a sudden, he was dizzy with fear. Mark was in hospital.

Oh, God. He shouldn't have left. He should never have left ...

"That's right, "the old woman went on. "I saw the ambulance come this morning. I always said that Jim was ripe for a heart attack. *You work too hard*, I'd say. But did he listen to me?"

"Mark's dad had a heart attack?" Ben cut in before she could keep going.

"Oh, yes, dear. Didn't I say? I heard all the ambulance sirens, so of course I looked out. I knew right away they were here for Jim."

She kept talking, but Ben tuned her out. The only thing that sank in at first was that Mark was OK. He hadn't been hurt in the fire.

Mark was OK – but his dad wasn't. The gremlin had struck again.

All of a sudden, Ben felt faint. Mark's dad hadn't even seen the statue. If the curse could go after him, who else could it target? How many more people were at risk?

He had to destroy the statue. He didn't know how, but he had to. No one was safe until the gremlin was gone.

The old woman was still rambling on. Ben hadn't heard a word of it.

"Sorry, I've got to go," he blurted out. He turned and ran for home.

It was too hot for running, but his panic drove him on. He was soaked in sweat by the time he got to the house. He didn't dare waste a single second. The curse could strike again at any time.

He had to find some way to end it. If he sold the statue, he'd only pass the curse on. So he had to break it. Smash it. Make sure the things inside it were gone for good.

But how?

Ben let himself in with his key. "Hello?" he called out, just in case. There was no one at home.

Even Tiger didn't seem to be in the house. Ben was glad. At least if things went wrong no one else would be hurt.

Of course, before his plan could go wrong, he needed to have one.

He dropped his bag on the hall floor. As he pulled out the statue, it seemed to smirk up at him. He was sure it was daring him to do his worst.

There had to be some way to destroy it.

Ben looked around, and his eyes fell on the tool kit in the corner.

Fire hadn't worked. Sea water hadn't worked. Maybe he should just smash it.

He picked up a hammer.

Chapter 11
A Crazy Idea

Ben didn't dare hold the statue down to hit it. He'd hammer his fingers for sure. Instead he took it out to the shed.

His dad had a vice that he used when he was doing woodwork. Ben turned the handle to clamp the statue in place.

"Right," he said out loud, his voice shaking a little. "Let's see you get out of that."

He raised the hammer, and took a swing.

The clang was so loud, Ben felt it in his teeth. He could swear that he saw a spark fly. But the statue didn't seem to be harmed. He gritted his teeth, and hit it again. And again. And again ...

The statue was slipping. He put the hammer down and reached for the handle of the vice. Which way did he have to turn it to tighten it? He couldn't remember.

He guessed wrong. He turned the handle the wrong way, and the statue dropped out. It would have hit his foot, but he was ready for it. As soon as he saw it start to fall, he jumped back.

That was his mistake.

He was too close to the wall. His head hit it with a terrible crack, and the air was pushed out of his lungs. Ben swayed and moved away, clutching his head.

He grabbed at a shelf for support, but it wasn't screwed down. As Ben pulled at it, the other end of the shelf went up in the air. Tools started to slide down towards him. Ben slapped his hand on the nearest one to stop it falling.

It was a saw, and he'd grabbed it by the blade.

For a moment, he just didn't believe what he'd done. He stared at his hand in shock as blood welled from the gash. He felt like he was going to faint.

But if he fainted, he was dead. He had to stop the bleeding now.

Ben sucked in a deep breath, and tried to wrap the hand up in his shirt. It wasn't enough to stop the bleeding. He needed a proper bandage.

First aid kit. There was a first aid kit in the kitchen. He left the shed and lurched back to the house. His head was still throbbing, and he thought he might puke.

It was hard to think in his panic. Where was the kit? He knew he'd used it only two days ago. It was in one of these cupboards ...

He threw things out on the floor as he hunted. It had to be here! Where was it, where was it ...?

He found the kit. Ben shook everything out onto the floor. What if there wasn't a bandage in there?

There was, but it took three tries to wrap his hand up. The fact that he was shaking didn't help. When he was done, he sat on the floor and panted for breath.

He was OK. It was under control. He wasn't going to bleed to death.

But he could have done – easily. What if he had fainted? Or cut his fingers off? Or the saw had fallen on his head? He'd been mad to try and smash the statue. It was far too dangerous.

Ben stood up slowly. He felt like he'd been in a punch-up. He had cuts and bruises all over. And he'd only had the statue a few days! What state would he be in by the end of the week?

He started to pick up the things he'd dumped on the floor. It hurt to move, but he didn't dare just leave them. The next time he tripped over could be his last.

One of the things he'd tipped out was a jam-jar full of coins. It was heavy, and he lifted it with care. He was sure if he dropped it, it would land on his foot.

Was this how he had to live now? Afraid of a jar full of money? Ben shook his head, and went to shove it in the cupboard.

Then he froze.

The jar had once been full of jam. Now it was full of coins and that seemed normal. Once the coins were dropped in there, it seemed like the jam jar was where they belonged.

Ben had just had a crazy idea.

He stared down at the jar in his hands. Could it work? Could it really be so simple?

There was only one way to find out.

He took the jar and headed out to the shed.

Chapter 12
Sold

The statue was still lying on the floor. Its mouth was open a bit and it looked very smug. Ben just picked it up and shoved it in his bag. He set off at a jog for the woods.

There was a pond in the local woods that the kids called the Pit. No one was sure how deep it was. There was a rumour that some little kid had drowned there once. Ben didn't know if that was true, but he knew no one went in the water. If he dropped the statue in, it wouldn't be found.

The problem was making sure it stayed there.

He reached the pond, and got the statue out of his bag. He used a twig to keep its mouth wedged open. He'd cut his fingers badly enough for one day.

Ben shook the jar of coins. How much money would it take? There was no way to guess. He'd just have to tip the whole lot in and hope.

He poured the coins into the statue. They seemed to make too much noise as they fell in. It was like he was dropping them down a long, deep well.

One of the last few coins got stuck against the twig. He wasn't stupid enough to poke at it. Instead, he gave the statue a tap on the head.

Its mouth snapped shut. The twig was crushed to splinters, and the coin cut clean in half.

"OK," Ben said. His heart was racing. "You made your point."

The gremlin was playing with him.

But maybe that was a good sign. If it knew what he was doing, then he could talk to it. He just hoped that it would listen to him.

"All right, gremlin," he said out loud. "You need someone to buy you? Well, now you've got money of your own. Pay your own price. I don't own you any more. Now – leave!"

With that, he threw the statue into the Pit.

It sank a whole lot slower than when Ben had thrown it into the sea. The head was the last part to go under the surface. Just before it did, Ben could swear he saw its smile grow wider.

He stood and waited for more of a sign, but there was none. Had the gremlin taken his offer? He didn't know.

It was a long, hot, slow walk home. By the time he got in, he was so tired he could die. But he knew he couldn't rest just yet.

Ben emptied his bag out on the hall floor. There was no sign of the statue.

He checked all the downstairs rooms. He checked the back garden. He even went back out to the shed.

Still no statue.

With his heart thumping, Ben went up the stairs. What would he do if it was up there waiting for him? This had been his last chance. If it hadn't worked ...

The fear was so strong that he had to shut his eyes. He made his way to the desk in his room by feel. Was it a good sign that he didn't trip over anything? Or was the gremlin playing tricks on him again?

He didn't want to look, but he had to. Slowly, Ben opened his eyes.

The statue was not on his desk. But something else was.

Five coins lay in a neat line. They were all twenty pence pieces. One pound in total.

The same price he'd paid for the statue.

Ben picked one of the coins up and stared at it. It was real, all right. He closed his hand around it. "Sold!" he said to the empty room.

Then his legs gave out, and he sat down hard on the floor.

It was over.

He sat there for a long time, in a daze. It was only when his mobile rang that he snapped out of it.

The phone was still on the hall floor where he'd dumped it. He picked it up, and saw that the number was Mark's.

"Hello?" He sat down on the stairs as he hit 'answer'.

"Ben! Hi. Did you try to call me earlier? I had to switch my phone off. I'm at the hospital." Mark sounded a bit shaken.

"I know, I heard." Ben's good mood drained away in an instant. How could he have forgotten? "Is your dad OK?"

"Yeah, he's ... he's fine." Mark let out a nervous laugh. "It was crazy! I'm telling you! It was a bit scary for a while there, and my dad wasn't doing so well. Then, all of a sudden, he's just ... fine! Sitting up in bed and asking what's going on. The doctors are going nuts."

"I bet they are." Ben could feel a grin spreading across his face. "So he's going to be all right?" He already knew what the answer would be.

He still had one of the coins from the desk in his hand. As he listened to Mark, he tossed it up and caught it.

It came up heads, five times in a row. Ben smiled to himself.

It looked like he was due for some good luck.

Barrington Stoke would like to thank all its readers for commenting on the manuscript before publication and in particular:

Alison Ball
Nicole Brogan
Amy Crawford
Gary Docherty
David Ferrel
Gill Ferris
David Gardiner
André Gauci
Craig Gray
Matthew Hamilton
Jodie Manley
Ashlee Maver
Blaine McKeever

Jessica Meek
Patrick John Mullins
Hayley Murray
Jill Peffers
Craig Ritchie
Paul Robertson
Chelsea Rutherford
Kris Rylance
Gary Smillie
Alan Summers
Steven Tully
Penny Ward

Become a Consultant!

Would you like to give us feedback on our titles before they are published? Contact us at the email address below – we'd love to hear from you!

info@barringtonstoke.co.uk
www.barringtonstoke.co.uk

More exciting titles ...

Snakebite

Mark is the boss on the estate. He thinks Alex has grassed him up. Mark isn't happy.

Now Alex is hunted, trapped – and on his own. After all, Mark is the boss, and Alex is a loser with only a pet snake to talk to.

Get out of that one, Snake Boy ...

You can order **Snakebite** directly from our website at **www.barringtonstoke.co.uk**

More exciting titles ...

Snapshot

Click. That's how easy it is. To take a photo. To change your life.

Victor didn't mean to get involved. But now he's taken photos of a crime. And someone wants those photos back. *Bad.*

You vs Them. You know the streets. He knows there's a gun in his jacket. With a bullet. Just for you. Can Victor manage to stay alive?

You can order **Snapshot** directly from our website at
www.barringtonstoke.co.uk

ST COLUMBA'S HIGH SCHOOL